RACHEL

Written and Illustrated by

Jackie McDonald

NEWMAN SPRINGS PUBLISHING
320 Broad Street
Red Bank, NJ 07701

First originally published by Newman Springs Publishing 2024

ISBN 979-8-89061-533-6 (Paperback)
ISBN 979-8-89061-534-3 (Digital)

Printed in the United States of America

I would like to dedicate my book to my family for encouraging me to be creative and be myself.

Rachel was getting ready for bed. She knew it was Monday night, and the *Billy the Clown* show was on.

Her mom was busy getting the baby changed, so Rachel turned the television on herself.

She had a hard time turning the channels but found the show she wanted. *Billy the Clown* was her favorite show!

Billy the Clown looked different to Rachel. She noticed that he had red hair and freckles. She turned the television off and went upstairs to bed.

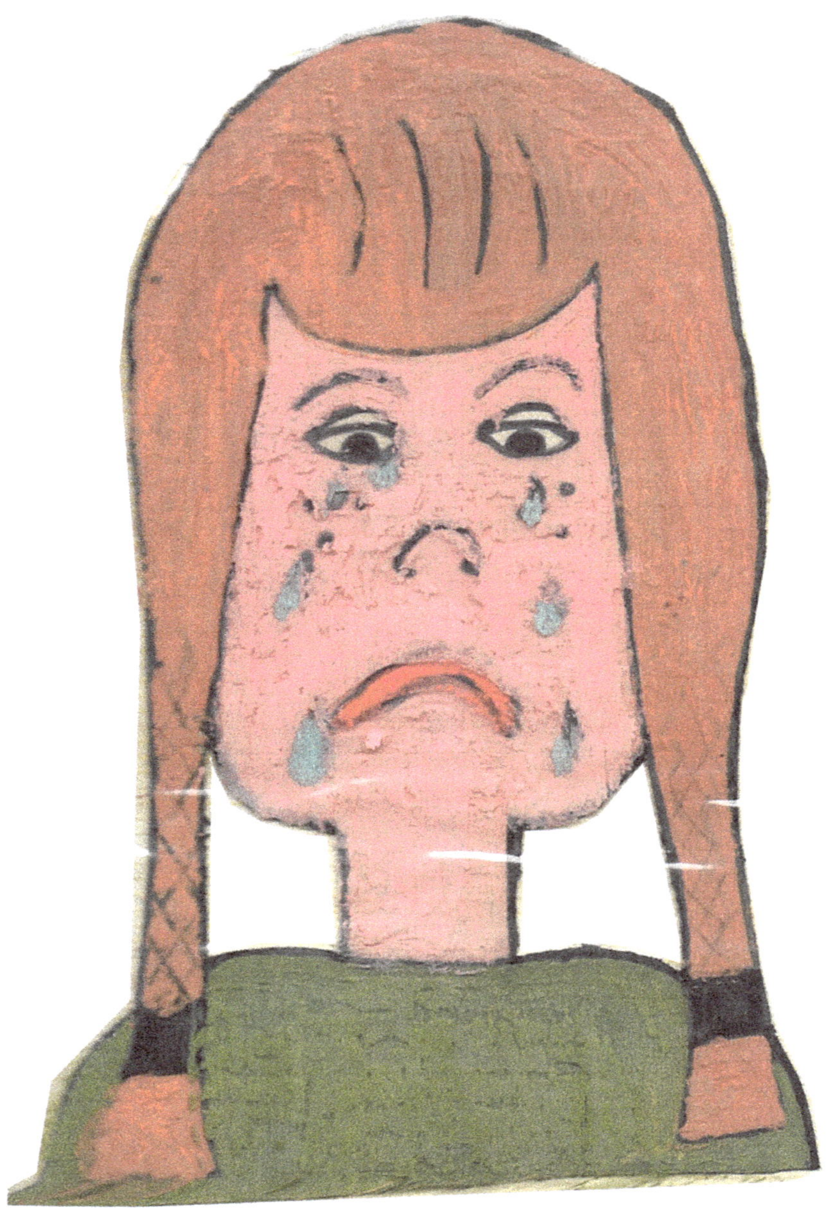

Rachel's mom and dad came to say good night and saw Rachel was crying. "What's wrong, honey?"

Rachel explained that Billy the Clown had red hair and freckles and so did she.

Rachel's mom and dad told her that a lot of people have red hair.

"Everyone is different," said her dad. Some people are short, some are tall. Some are big, and some are small.

"I have red hair, and your mom loves me!"

"It's only a color, and we both love you and your red hair."

"I'm sure you will find a new friend with red hair when you start school tomorrow."

The next day at school, Rachel looked around the room.

She saw that all the children were different. Some had freckles, but nobody had red hair.

Rachel felt sad until the teacher walked in. She looked up and smiled.

The teacher had brownish-red hair and freckles.

Now Rachel felt a little bit better.

Soon it was picture time, and Rachel met a boy named Jimmy. The teacher asked everyone to draw a picture of their family and friends.

Rachel drew her family, but when she went to use the brown crayon for her mom's hair, they were all gone. All the children were coloring the hair black, brown, and yellow.

CRAYONS
CRAYONS
CRAYONS

Now she was sad again but finished her picture.

Her new friend, Jimmy, came over to her and showed her his picture. It was a picture of himself and his new friend, Rachel.

Rachel really liked the picture and felt special.

Today was a good day for Rachel because she was happy she had red hair and a new friend!

ABOUT THE AUTHOR

Jackie has always worked with children including twenty years at the school board. Jackie enjoys books and art and loves writing. Jackie hopes you enjoy the book and it leaves you smiling.